The Dance

The Dance

Anna-Stina Johansson

Sandra looked up from her book and couldn't believe her eyes! Was he really coming in her direction? Adam, the cute boy that just had been transferred to her class to help the school's football team to win. She pinched herself in the arm to make sure she wasn't dreaming. She wasn't. This was real. He actually made his way, through the dancing couples, towards her where she sat alone on the bench.

She had never been asked to dance when they had had dance classes in the school's gymnasium. Why she didn't know. Or maybe she did. Her aunt had told her that it was because she was tall, taller than most of her classmates. She didn't believe that that was the reason because there were a couple of other girls who were just as tall and they were always asked to dance. Sandra herself believed that it was because her nose was slightly bent, just right on that spot where you hold your fingers to stop a nose bleed. She knew she was ugly. She didn't care that she had long nice hair and a slender body. No, her nose was awful.

Now he was standing in front of her. Did he need glasses? Couldn't he see that she wasn't beautiful? Why did he reach out his hand to her? He must be insane!

"Shall we dance?" he said and gave her a warm smile.

He obviously hadn't learned all the rules on this high school, such as the secret rule that no one should ever ask her to dance. Everybody else, except her, was asked to dance. These school dances made Sandra so furious! She was a bright student. The teachers liked having her in the class. She knew the answers and was eager to learn more. But during dancing class she felt like the ugliest person in the world with no skills at all. That's why she had started to bring a book. It made her feel less lonely.

And here he was, Adam, asking her to dance. Sandra opened her mouth but then shut it again. She looked down at her book.

He crouched down. "I've never been turned down before." He gently put his hand under her chin and lifted it so that she had to look at him. "I guess I must have lost my touch since I can't compete with a book." His eyes

twinkled.

She flushed, didn't know where to look. In

the corner of her eye she noticed how the

others glowered at her. Couldn't he go

away! Didn't he understand how

embarrassing this was for her? Still, she

liked having his attention.

"What is it about?" He sounded genuinely

interested.

"The World War II, when the atomic bomb

hit Hiroshima."

"Oh, for English class. I haven't started reading it yet." He made a face. "Didn't we get a few weeks to finish it?"

"Yes, but I don't have anything better to do."

"Yes you do." He took her book and placed it on the bench. Rose. Grabbed her by her hands and dragged her out on the dance floor. He grinned at her. "Dancing is better than reading."

"But...but...I'm no good at this..." She felt sweat on her palms.

He held her hands between his and patted

her left hand. "Don't worry, I'll show you."

Her cheeks turned red but she didn't care

about that at all. Instead she smiled because

that was the cutest gesture she had ever

seen! Sandra couldn't explain why but it felt

so good that he, the popular one, cared

about her. Then she thought she was going

to die of embarrassment when he placed

her arms on his shoulders. He had such

muscular arms! When he put his hands on

her waist Sandra stopped breathing for a

while. This was the first time ever that she

had gotten a tickling feeling inside when

someone touched her.

A new song started but her feelings made it

hard for her to concentrate on the steps.

Then it happened, she stepped on his foot.

Oh no, he must think that she was the most

clumsy girl in the world!

Once again he lifted her chin. "No worries,"

he smiled. "It'll be much easier if you look

into my eyes while we dance."

Sandra took a deep breath before she let

their eyes meet. And yes, he was right,

indeed it became easier. He made her feel

like a fairy that was floating in the air. His eyes were divine and she smiled. But wait, why did he grin at her?

He bent his head. "Thanks," he whispered in her ear.

"Oh dear, I actually said it loud!"

"Feel free to share your thoughts with me anytime you like." He pulled her closer. Sandra thought that her heart was going to pop out of her chest when she felt his hard body against hers. It felt like she was in heaven. But she was abruptly brought back to now when the music faded out and an elbow jabbed her side. Sandra almost tripped.

"The next dance is mine." The haughty girl from the popular group stepped into Adam's arms and turned her back on Sandra.

Sandra felt like a homeless dog that had been shouted at. She went tail-between-her-legs back to the bench, grabbed her book and left.

*

The following day her humiliation had settled. She kicked the stones that were lying on the sidewalk. Damn all these popular people who thought they were better than everybody else! The gray clouds started to close in overhead and the thunder rumbled in the distance. Oh just great, it would probably be raining cats and dogs by the time she got to school! She kicked a stone as far as she could. A red car passed her and then it suddenly stopped, like it was waiting for her to catch up. It intimidated her a bit so she started walking faster. When she was beside the car she recognized the driver. It was Adam.

"Hey you, get in the car before you get all wet."

"You don't have to care about that!" She started walking again. The first raindrop landed on her nose.

He drove slowly besides her. "Sandra, don't be so stubborn. Get in now will you!"

Stubborn! Who was he to call her that? Her eyes flashed. "I'd rather get soaked than ride in a car with you!"

"Can't you please let me explain about yesterday?"

"No!" What was there to explain? That she was made a fool of as usual. And that she made a fool of herself by letting him know that she liked him. She didn't want to hear him say that he was only interested in her as a friend. For once in her life she wanted more than just being friends. But he probably just wanted to charm her in order to get help with the homework. That was the story of her life. She was good enough to help people with their homework but nothing else. Today she decided to put an end to that! And she had had it in over her ears with all the people who had used her during the years. Enough was enough! And here he was coming with his fancy car, imagining that she would see him as a knight on a white horse that came rescuing her from getting wet. What a fool he was!

"Please, it feels like I'm getting blamed for what others have done to you."

"I don't care."

"But I do. Please, let me prove that I'm nothing like them!" The thunder almost drowned his voice.

Sandra stopped. It was drizzling now. She hesitated before she opened her mouth.

"Fair enough."

Adam smiled and stopped the car.

When she reached for the door handle another car slowed down, it was a couple of people from the popular group. One of them leaned out through the window and yelled. "Hey Adam, if you want to get new friends you can do better than that trailer tramp!" Their laughter made Sandra run as fast as she could into the trees. In the background she could hear Adam start swearing.

Finally she reached her favorite spot, a big oak-tree next to the pond. She didn't care that it probably wasn't the best idea to sit under an oak if lightning struck, but she figured that it had probably stood there for hundred years so why would anything happen to it right now? And who would miss her? The rain was pouring down now, it started to seep through the leafage and make her wet. Adam now knew where she came from. What a fool she was that thought that she could keep it a secret. It was just that that he was the first guy she really liked and she didn't want him to know about her background. That her father was in prison for robbery and that her mother had two jobs but still couldn't afford to live anywhere else. But she adored her mother who always made sure that Sandra and her two sisters had plenty to eat, fresh clothes and a roof over their heads. She knew that her mother did the best she could but still she was embarrassed for living in a trailer park.

She pulled up her knees against her body, leaned her head on them and cried. She thought about the dance, when Adam had patted her hand, it had felt so nice! But he would never do that again. Not now. What good did it do that she was a straight A student? That didn't make her popular and it certainly didn't erase her background. She would always be the trailer girl, the daughter of a robber. But yet she couldn't help to feel proud that she did so well in school despite the fact that she most of the time had to babysit her sisters and do the housework. She wondered if Adam would be impressed by that, but probably not. Why would he? The school had started now but for the first time in her life she didn't bother about going there. She actually wished that her beloved oak would get hit by the lightning.

Suddenly she flinched. What was that? Had someone called her name?

"Sandra, where are you?"

She wasn't imagining it. Someone was actually out there looking for her in this weather!

"Sandra!"

Adam. What would she do? Run to him and let him sweep her off her feet like in a fairytale? She smiled. No, what was she thinking. That was absolutely out of the question! Then she sneezed.

"Sandra, are you there?"

She tried to hold back another sneeze but couldn't.

"Bless you!" He peered around the trunk and gave her a warm smile. "Finally I found you!" Once again he crouched down in front of her. "So this is your secret spot? You

shouldn't be sitting here in this weather."

"Go away!" Sandra turned around and

looked at the raindrops that were running

down the tree trunk. She didn't want him to

see that she'd been crying.

He looked puzzled. "Weren't you about to

give me a second chance?"

She shrugged. "Maybe I've changed my

mind about that."

"I don't believe you." Adam grabbed her by

the shoulders and turned her around. "I

won't go anywhere until you've heard my side of the story!"

"Fine." Sandra sighed. "Go ahead, but I know what kind of guy you are."

"No you don't." He touched her arm. "If you had stayed yesterday you would have seen that I didn't dance with her. First I felt that I had to since she threatened to make my life a living hell here if I didn't dance with her. That's why I didn't come after you."

She looked up. Their eyes met.

"You see, for one moment I believed her, since she knows many of my team mates and I wanted just like everybody else to fit in. I hated myself for thinking like that when I saw the look on your face. However, when I came to my senses you were already gone."

She could tell that he wasn't lying. "I had no idea." She bit her lip. "I guess I jumped into the wrong conclusion. I'm so sorry."

"Apology accepted," he smiled.

The storm had passed but a chilly breeze made Sandra shiver.

"Are you freezing?"

She nodded.

Then Adam grabbed her by the arms and pulled her up on the feet. "You're all wet. Take off your blouse." He started to unbutton his shirt.

She just stood there staring at him.

Adam grinned. "You'll get sick otherwise. Here take my shirt at least it's not as wet as your blouse."

Huh. Her eyes narrowed.

"You know my shirt is made of fleece so I can guarantee that it's better than what you're wearing now. Don't worry, I'll turn around and I promise not to peep."

She blushed. "Are you a mind reader?"

He laughed heartily. "No, but it wasn't too hard to guess what you were thinking."

Sandra took his shirt and then he turned around. She found herself staring at his broad shoulders. What was happening to her? It seemed like every time he was around her she got absorbed by him. Maybe he had put a spell on her.

"So is it safe for me to face you now?"

"Yes." She blushed once again when their eyes met.

Adam noticed her teary eyes. "They aren't worth your tears."

She looked down. He took one step closer and embraced her. She almost didn't dare to breathe against his bare skin. His warmth made her troubles go away. She smiled when she realized that his heart too was beating faster. This was more than she ever could have dreamed of! He actually liked her despite everything. Was he from another planet? She giggled. By now he was laughing. Oh no!

"Did I think loud again?"

"Yes dear, you did, but don't worry about that." He stroked her hair.

"That's easy for you to say! I don't want you to know every thought I have. That's embarrassing!"

"No it's not, it's just cute." He bent down and kissed her on the head. "What do you say? Shall we go back to school, hand in hand, to give them something to talk about?"

She took a step back. "Are you crazy? I would never dare to do that!"

"Sure you do. I'll be there holding your hand every step of the way."

"But have you forgotten what they shouted?"

"No, but that's their opinion and not mine. I like you just the way you are."

Her heart melted. "I guess we can do that if you promise to not let go."

"I promise." And then he kissed her hand.

"You do understand that a lot of questions are spinning around in my head, right?"

"Yes, but I think that your biggest problem is that you think way too much. For once, try to follow your intuition and don't bother about other people. Can you please try and do that for me?" He stroked her hair behind her ear.

She shivered by his touch. Okay, we better go now before I lose my nerve and before I want to rip off all of your clothes she thought and could barely take her eyes off from his tummy.

Adam got a twinkle in his eye. "So you want to see me naked?"

Sandra could barely speak of embarrassment. "You must indeed be a sorcerer that has put a spell on me since all my thoughts come out loud when I'm around you."

He burst out to laughter. "Well, I'm not. I'm just a caring guy that enjoys being around you. Is that okay with you?"

"Yes." Now she too smiled.

"Good." He reached out his hand. "So do you feel ready to meet the world with me?"

"Yes." Sandra took his hand and for the first time she felt that she could conquer anything because now she had someone who believed in her.

www.ingramcontent.com/pod-product-compliance
Lightning Source LLC
Chambersburg PA
CBHW071228130626
46555CB00004B/1892